This book belongs to:

_____

A DORLING KINDERSLEY BOOK

Managing Editor   Bridget Gibbs
Managing Art Editor   Chris Fraser
Editor   Fiona Munro
Designer   Lisa Hollis
Photography   Steve Gorton
DTP Designer   Kim Browne
Production   Katy Holmes

Rhymes selected by Shona McKellar

First published in hardback in 1998
by Dorling Kindersley Limited,
9 Henrietta St, London WC2E 8PS
Paperback edition published in 1999

www.dk.com

ISBN: 0-7513-7202-1 (paperback alone)
0-7513-7141-6 (paperback with tape)

Colour reproduction by Colourscan
Printed in Singapore by Tien Wah Press

A CIP catalogue record for this book is available from the British Library.

Dorling Kindersley would like to thank the following for appearing in this book:
Jake George-Samuels, Rebekah Murrell, Sarah and Harry Hayden,
Merryl, Phoebe and Martha Epstein, Hideyuki and Amané Sobue,
Freya Hartas, Alison and Harriet Hunter, Neeraj and Naveena Kapur,
Bindi Haria, Sally and Jake Davies, Alex Squire Melmoth,
Shanti Gorton, Raphael Cox, Caitlin and Madeleine Hennessy.

Playtime Rhymes

for the Very Young

Illustrated by Priscilla Lamont

DORLING KINDERSLEY

LONDON • NEW YORK • SYDNEY • MOSCOW

Contents

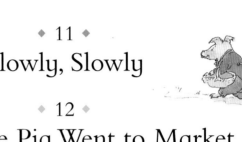

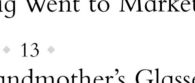

Knock at the Door

Knock on forehead

Knock at the door,

Lift eyebrow

Peep in,

Pull ear

Ring the bell,

Push nose up

Lift the latch,

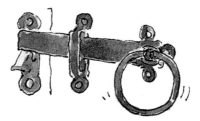

Put finger in mouth

And walk in.

I Saw a Slippery, Slithery Snake

I saw a slippery, slithery snake

Slide through the grasses,
making them shake.

Weave hands from side to side

He looked at me
with his beady eye.

Circle eyes

"Go away from my
pretty green garden," said I.

Go away!

"Sssss," said the slippery, slithery snake

As he slid through the grasses,
making them shake.

Repeat first action

9

Round and Round the Garden

Round and round the garden,
Like a teddy bear.
One step, two steps,
Tickly under there.

Round and round the haystack,
Went the little mouse.
One step, two steps,
In this little house.

Circle palm

Walk fingers up…

baby's arm and…

tickle!

Slowly, Slowly

Slowly, slowly, very slowly
Creeps the garden snail.
Slowly, slowly, very slowly
Up the wooden rail.

Walk hand...

slowly up...

baby's...

tummy

Quickly, quickly, very quickly
Runs the little mouse.
Quickly, quickly, very quickly
Round about the house.

Tickle baby throughout second verse

11

This Little Pig Went to Market

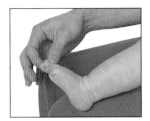

Wiggle…

This little pig
went to market,

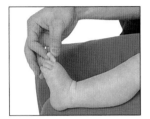

each…

This little pig
stayed at home,

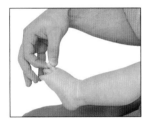

toe…

This little pig
had roast beef,

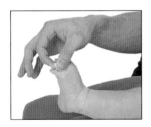

in…

This little pig
had none,

And this little
pig cried

turn

Wee-wee-wee

Tickle!

All the way home.

These are Grandmother's Glasses

These are Grandmother's glasses,
This is Grandmother's hat;
Grandmother claps her hands like this,
And rests them in her lap.

These are Grandfather's glasses,
This is Grandfather's hat;
Grandfather folds his arms like this,
And has a little nap.

See-Saw, Margery Daw

Rock backwards and forwards

See-saw, Margery Daw,

Johnny shall have a new master,

He shall have but a penny a day,

Because he can't work any faster.

See-saw, Jack in the hedge,

Which is the way to London Bridge?

Put on your shoes and away you trudge,

That is the way to London Bridge.

Here's a Ball for Baby

Here's a ball for baby,
Big and fat and round.

Here is baby's hammer,
See how it can pound.

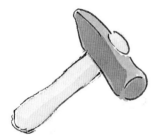

Here are baby's soldiers,
Standing in a row.

Here is baby's music,
Clapping, clapping so.

Jelly on the Plate

Rock from side to side

Jelly on the plate,
Jelly on the plate,
Wibble wobble,
Wibble wobble,
Jelly on the plate.

Sweeties in the jar,
Sweeties in the jar,
Shake them up,
Shake them up,
Sweeties in the jar.

Bounce up and down

Blow!

Candles on the cake,
Candles on the cake,
Blow them out,
Blow them out,
Puff puff puff!

16

Incy Wincy Spider

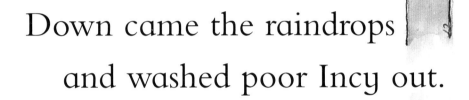

Incy Wincy spider
   climbed up the water spout,

Touch index fingers and thumbs in turn by twisting wrists

Down came the raindrops
   and washed poor Incy out.

Raise hands and wiggle fingers as you lower

Out came the sunshine
   and dried up all the rain,

Raise hands and make a wide circle with arms

Incy Wincy spider
   climbed up the spout again.

Repeat first action

Two Little Dicky Birds

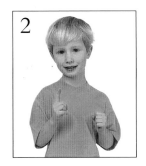

Two little dicky birds
Sitting on a wall,

One named Peter,

One named Paul.

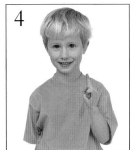

Fly away Peter!

Fly away Paul!

Come back Peter,

Come back Paul.

There's a Wide-Eyed Owl

There's a wide-eyed owl
With a pointed nose,
He has pointed ears
And claws for toes.
He sits in a tree
And looks at you,
Then flaps his wings and says,

"Tu-whit, tu-whoo!"

Flap   Flap

Five Little Peas

Five little peas in a pea-pod pressed,

One grew, two grew, and so did all the rest.

They grew…and grew…and did not stop,

Until one day the pod went…POP!

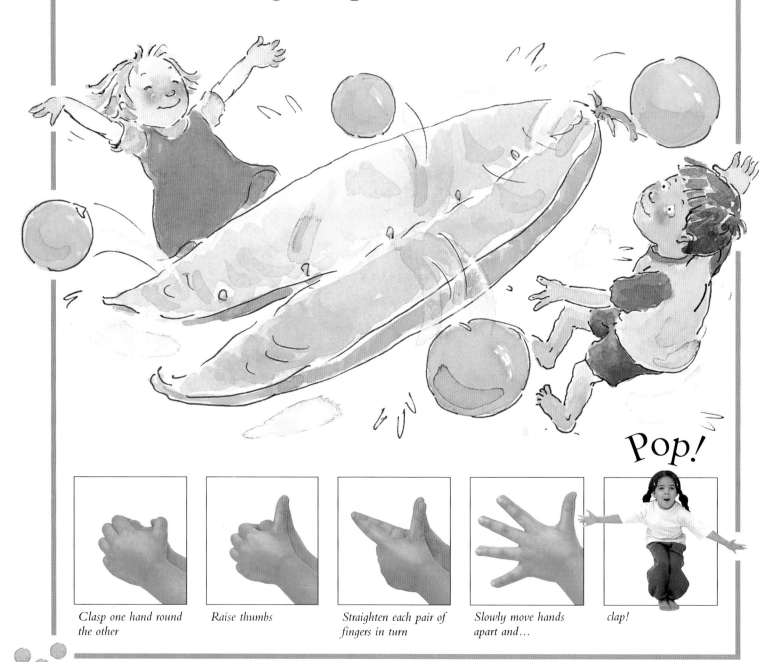

Pop!

Clasp one hand round the other

Raise thumbs

Straighten each pair of fingers in turn

Slowly move hands apart and…

clap!

20

Cobbler, Cobbler

Cobbler, cobbler, mend my shoe,

Get it done by half-past two,

'Cos my toe is peeping through,

Cobbler, cobbler, mend my shoe.

Bang fists together

Poke index finger through fingers of other hand

Repeat first action

What Do You Suppose?

What do you suppose?
A bee sat on my nose!

Then what do you think?
He gave me a wink,

And said, "I beg your pardon,
I thought you were the garden!"

Fly away, bee!

Pat-a-cake

Pat-a-cake, pat-a-cake, baker's man,

Bake me a cake as fast as you can.

Pat it and prick it and mark it with B,

And put it in the oven
for Baby and me.

Clap in rhythm 　　*'Pat' and 'prick' baby's hand* 　　*Trace 'B'* 　　*Slide cake into oven*

Two Little Men in a Flying Saucer

Two little men in a flying saucer

Flew round the world one day.

Move baby's arms up and down

Lift baby and move in a circle

They looked to the left and

right a bit,

Turn head to left and right

And couldn't bear the sight of it,

And then they flew away.

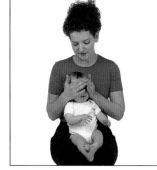
Cover eyes

Repeat first action

This is the Way the Ladies Ride

*Bounce baby, getting faster as rhyme progresses,
and lowering baby between knees at end*

This is the way the ladies ride,
Nimble-nim, nimble-nim.

This is the way the gentlemen ride,
Gallop-a-trot, gallop-a-trot.

This is the way the farmers ride,
Jiggety-jog, jiggety-jog.

This is the way the butcher boy rides,
Tripperty-trot, tripperty-trot,

Till he falls in a ditch with a flipperty,
Flipperty, flop, flop, FLOP!

Build a House with Five Bricks

Build a house with five bricks,
One, two, three, four, five.

Place fists on top of each other in turn

Make a roof

Put a roof on top,

And a chimney too,

Straighten arms for chimney

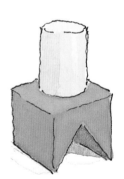

Blow!

Where the wind blows through!

whoo whoo

Here is the Church

Here is
the church,

Interlace fingers

Here is the steeple,

Point index fingers

Open the doors,

Open thumbs

And here are the people.

Turn hands over and wiggle fingertips

Here is the parson
going upstairs,

Walk fingers of one hand up fingers of other hand

And here he is
a-saying his prayers.

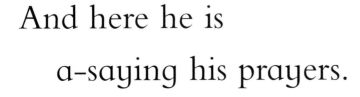

Pray

Hickory Dickory Dock

Clap three times

Hickory dickory dock,

The mouse
ran up the clock.

Walk fingers up arm

The clock
struck one,

Clap once

The mouse
ran down,

Walk fingers down arm

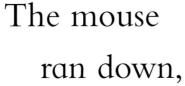

Hickory dickory dock.

Clap three times

The Baby in the Cradle

The baby in the cradle
Goes rock-a-rock-a-rock.

The clock on the dresser
Goes tick-a-tick-a-tock.

The rain on the window
Goes tap-a-tap-a-tap,

But here comes the sun,
So we clap-a-clap-a-clap!

Rock arms

Swing arm from side to side

Tap finger on hand

Clap three times